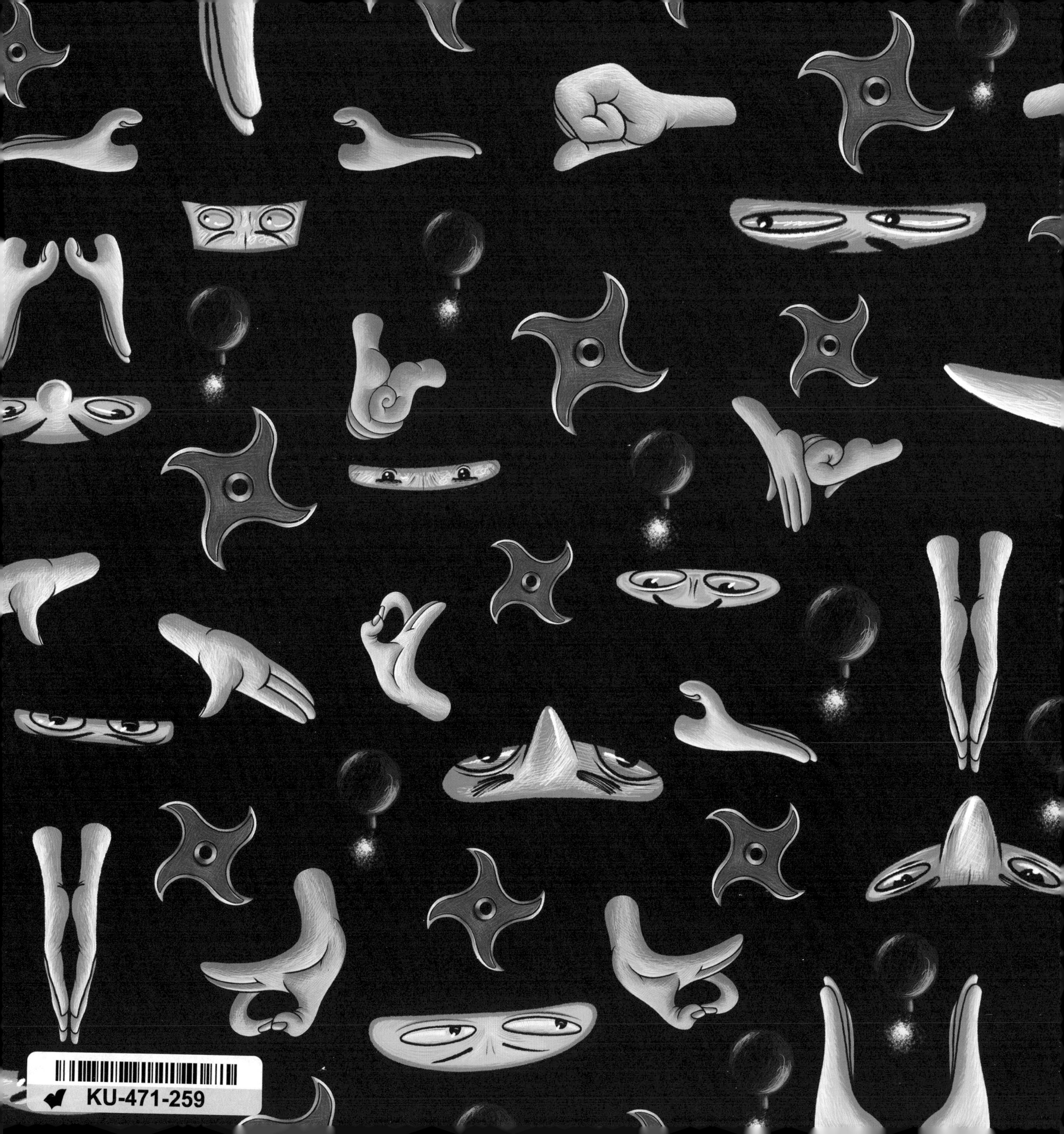

For Lorcan, my littlest ninja – MZ

For Leo – AW

Rita Wants a Ninja published by Graffeg in 2022.

ISBN 9781802580426

First published by An tSnáthaid Mhór Teoranta, 2019.

A CIP Catalogue record for this book is available from the British Library.

Mae Rita Eisiau Ninja (Welsh edition) ISBN 9781802580433
Rita agus an Ninja (Irish edition) ISBN 9781912929177

The publisher acknowledges the financial support of the Books Council of Wales. www.gwales.com.

Teaching Resources
www.graffeg.com/pages/teachers-resources

1 2 3 4 5 6 7 8 9

GRAFFEG

This book belongs to

____

____

____

____

Rita wants a Ninja

By Máire Zepf
Illustrated by Mr Ando

This is Rita.

Rita is playing hide-and-seek.

7

Rita wants a ninja.

A ninja is silent, fast,

and invisible.

A ninja master would teach Rita the art of invisibility.

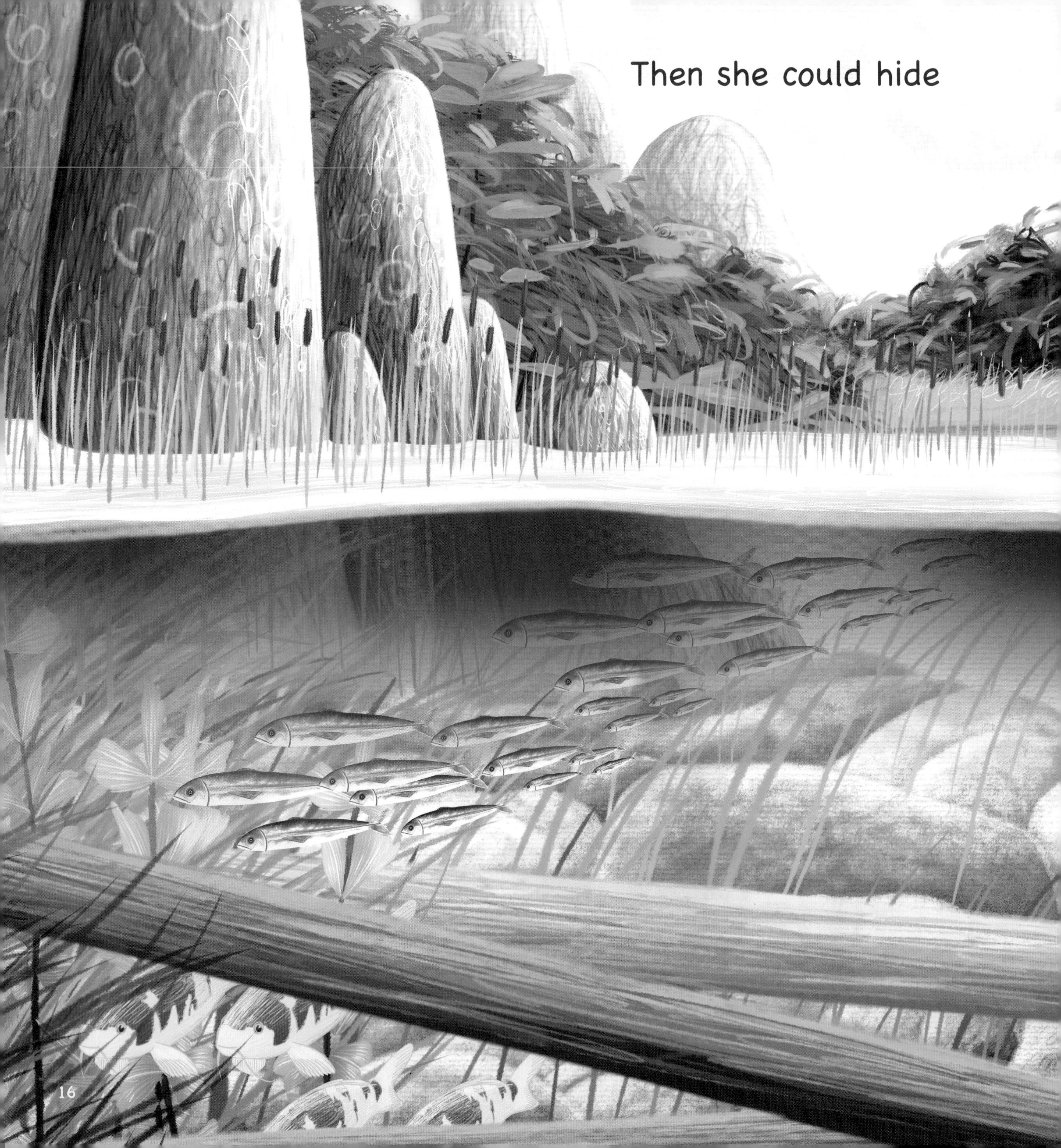

Then she could hide

and hide

and hide.

Rita would only be found when she wanted to be.

Then her ninja master
would train her.

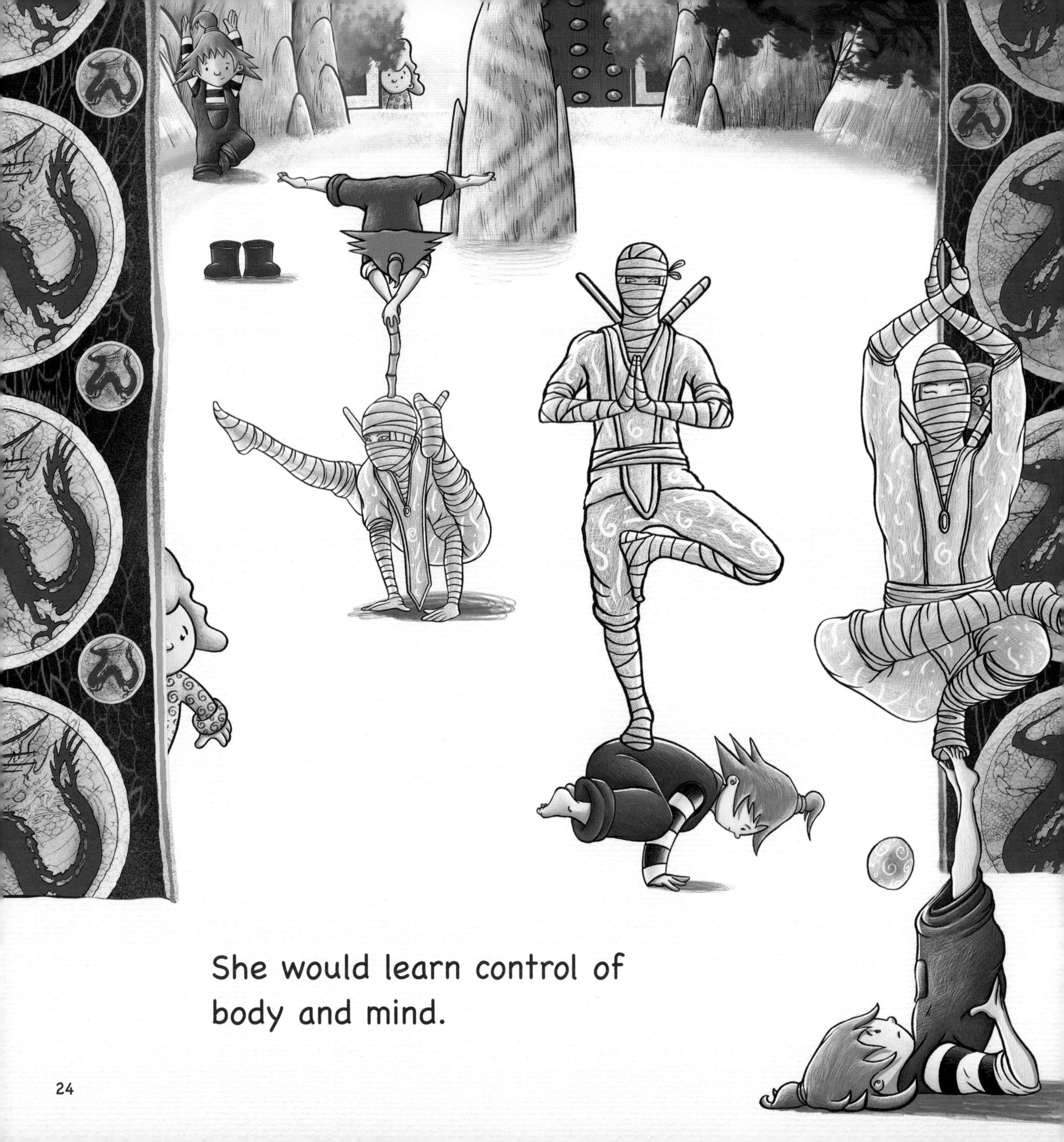

She would learn control of
body and mind.

She would learn
the art of ***HIIYAAAA!***
and ***KIAIIII!***

Rita would be
invincible.

But ninjas don't just
train and hide, do they?

Ninjas mean trouble.

Ninjas sneak.

And steal things.

And ninjas come with ninja clans.

And if that isn't bad enough,
ninjas love to fight.

Rita hates
fighting.

Where would it end?

Aa

aaaahhhhhhh!

No, Rita doesn't need a ninja master after all.

She'll be the master.
And she knows just the student.